THIS WALKER BOOK BELONGS TO:

_____

_____

_____

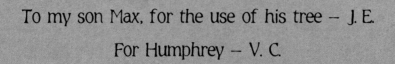

To my son Max, for the use of his tree — J. E.

For Humphrey — V. C.

First published 2001 by Walker Books Ltd, 87 Vauxhall Walk, London SE11 5HJ

This edition published 2002

13 15 17 19 20 18 16 14 12

Text © 2001 Jonathan Emmett
Illustrations © 2001 Vanessa Cabban

You can find out more about Jonathan Emmett's books
by visiting his website at www.scribblestreet.co.uk

This book has been typeset in Beta Bold

Printed in China

British Library Cataloguing in Publication Data:
a catalogue record for this book is available from the British Library

ISBN 978-0-7445-8950-4

www.walker.co.uk

Bringing Down the Moon

Jonathan Emmett   illustrated by Vanessa Cabban

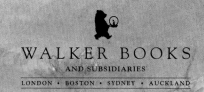

WALKER BOOKS
AND SUBSIDIARIES
LONDON · BOSTON · SYDNEY · AUCKLAND

"Hot-diggerty!" exclaimed Mole
as he burrowed out of the ground
one night. "Whatever's that?"

The moon was hanging in the sky
above him, like a bright silver coin.
Mole thought that it was the
most beautiful thing that
he had ever seen.

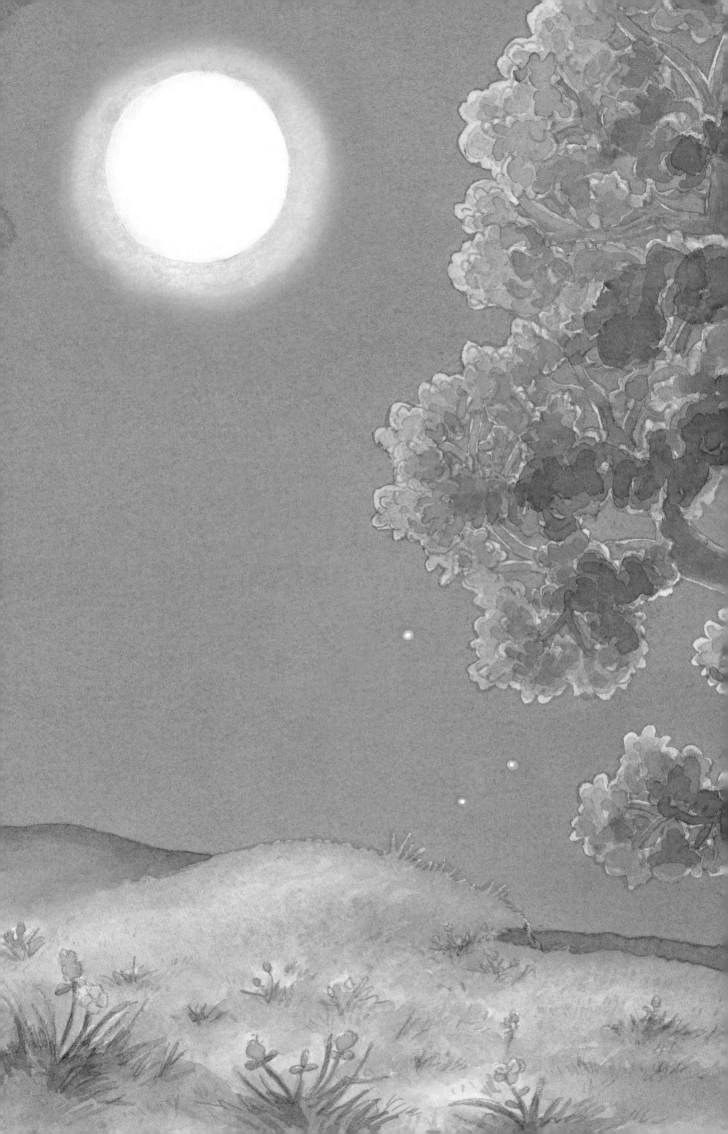

"Whatever it is,
I must have it,"
Mole said to
himself.
"I know. I'll
jump up and
pull it down."

THUMP-
THUMP!

THUMPETY-
BUMP!

Mole was so busy jumping he didn't think about the noise he was making, and he woke up Rabbit in her burrow.

"Mole!" said Rabbit. "What on earth do you think you're doing?"

"Hello, Rabbit," said Mole. "I'm trying to pull down that shiny thing."

"You mean the moon?" asked Rabbit.

"So that's what it's called," said Mole.

"You'll never do that," said Rabbit. "It's not as near as it looks."

But Mole would
not give up.
"I know," he thought.
"I'll get a stick
and poke it down."
He found a long
stick and poked it
up at the moon.

SWISH-
SWISH!

SWISHETY-
SWISH!

Mole was so
busy poking that
he tripped over
Hedgehog in
his bed of
leaves.

"Mole," grunted Hedgehog.
"What the weevil are you up to?"

"Hello, Hedgehog," said Mole,
"I'm trying to poke down the moon."

"You'll never do that," said Hedgehog.
"It's not as near as it looks."

But Mole would not give up.
"I know," he thought. "I'll throw
something at it and knock it down."
He found some acorns and threw
them at the moon.

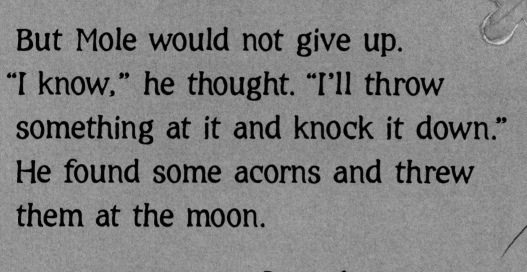

PLINK-PLINK!

PLINKETY-PLINK!

"Ouch!"
said Squirrel.
"Mole, have you gone nuts?"

"Hello, Squirrel," said Mole.
"I'm trying to knock down the moon."

"You'll never do that," said Squirrel.
"It's not as near as it looks."

But Mole wanted the moon
so badly, he would not give up.
"I know," he thought. "I'll climb
a tree and fetch it down!"

Mole had never climbed a
tree before. It was hard work
and he was scared to be so
far from the ground.
But he kept on going until
he saw the moon
resting in the leaves
above him.

Mole stretched out his paws. But just when he thought he had the moon ... he slipped!

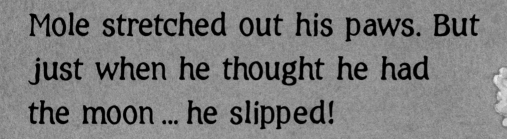

"Oh! Eeek! Ouch! Ooh!"

Mole tumbled down and landed

SPLASH!

in the middle of a puddle.

"Hot-dang-diggerty-drat!"
thought Mole. "I almost had it that time."
Then he noticed something
floating in the puddle beside him.
It was pale and wrinkled,
but Mole recognized
it at once.

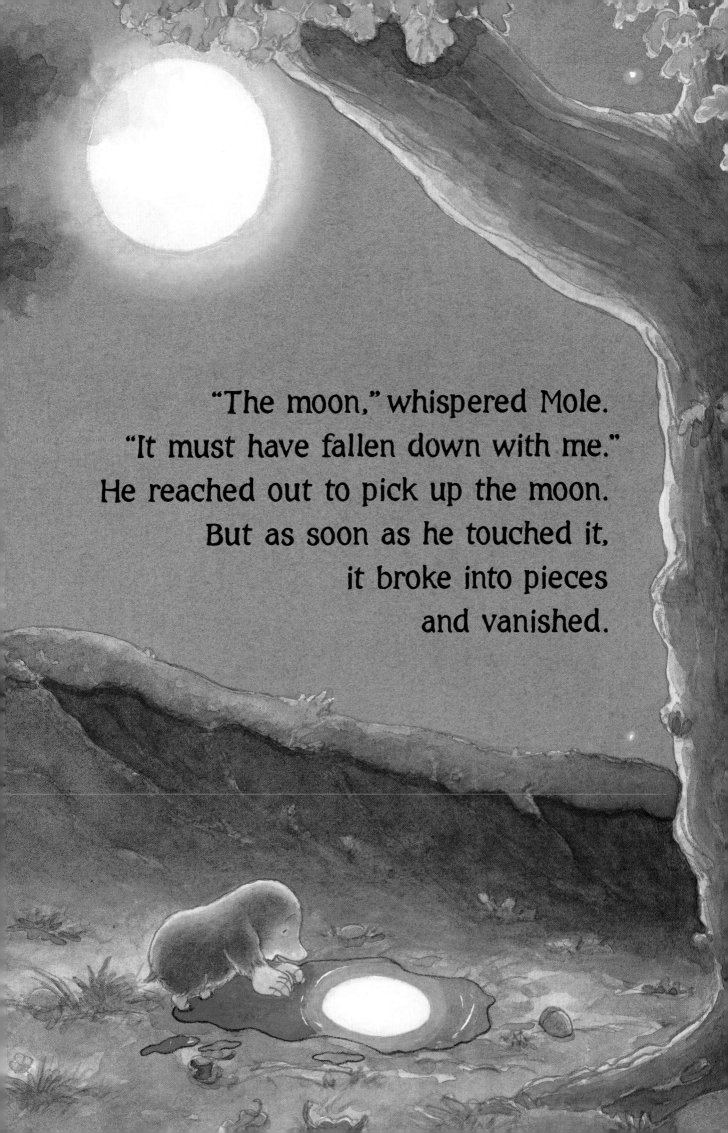

"The moon," whispered Mole.
"It must have fallen down with me."
He reached out to pick up the moon.
But as soon as he touched it,
it broke into pieces
and vanished.

Mole sat in the puddle and cried.
Rabbit, Hedgehog and Squirrel
came running up.
"Are you all right, Mole?"
asked Rabbit.

"I'm all right," sobbed Mole.
"But the moon isn't! I pulled it down,
and then I broke it, and it was
SO beautiful ... and now I shall
never see it again."

"Oh, Mole," said Rabbit,
"you couldn't have pulled down the moon."

"And you couldn't have broken it,"
said Hedgehog.

"And you'll certainly see it again,"
said Squirrel. "Look!"

High up in the sky above them, the moon
was coming out from behind a cloud.

"Oh," whispered Mole, "and it's
just as beautiful as ever."

Mole, Rabbit, Hedgehog and
Squirrel stood and stared up
at the moon together.

"It is beautiful," said Rabbit.

"Very beautiful!" said Hedgehog.

"Very beautiful indeed!"
said Squirrel.

"Yes,"
said Mole.
"But it's NOT
as near as
it looks!"

Meet the Mole who thinks a lot...

ISBN 978-1-4063-1957-6

Mole thinks that it is too wet outside to visit his friends so he decides to dig a tunnel to Rabbit's burrow. If there's one thing Mole's good at it's digging, but getting there is harder than he thinks.

Mole thinks his burrow is small, dark and dull. So he sets off to find somewhere big, bright and beautiful instead. But finding the perfect home is not that simple!

ISBN 978-1-84428-521-1

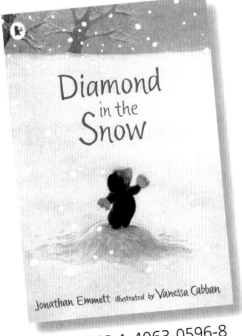

ISBN 978-1-4063-0596-8

Mole thinks the diamond he's found is magic. It appeared from nowhere, then it disappeared altogether. But sometimes things are not quite as they seem.

"Wonderful… Just right for joining in." *Carousel*